Octopus

by

Steve Yockey

IMPORTANT BILLING AND CREDIT REQUIREMENTS

All producers of *OCTOPUS* *must* give credit to the Author of the Play in all programs distributed in connection with performances of the Play, and in all instances in which the title of the Play appears for the purposes of advertising, publicizing or otherwise exploiting the Play and/ or a production. The name of the Author *must* appear on a separate line on which no other name appears, immediately following the title and *must* appear in size of type not less than fifty percent of the size of the title type.

Producing theatres must include the following billing in their programs: "Originally developed and produced by Actor's Express Theatre, Atlanta, Georgia, Freddie Ashley, Artistic Director, Zak Topor, Managing Director.

The World Premiere of ***OCTOPUS*** opened January 27, 2008 at the King Plow Arts Center in Atlanta, GA. Produced by Actor's Express Theatre Company with Artistic Director Freddie Ashley and Managing Director Zak Topor. Directed by Kate Warner.

Stage Manager . . . . Jude Futral
Scenic Design . . . . .Kat Conley
Lighting Design . . . . Joseph P. Monaghan
Sound Design . . . . Joseph P. Monaghan
Costume Design . . . . English Benning

With the following cast:
KEVIN . . . . Joe Sykes
BLAKE . . . . .Tony Larkin
MAX . . . . .John Benzinger
ANDY . . . . Mitchell Anderson
TELEGRAM DELIVERY BOY . . . . .Brian Crawford

The West Coast Premiere of ***OCTOPUS*** opened May 17, 2008 in the Magic Theatre's Sam Shepard Theater in San Francisco, CA. Co-produced by Encore Theatre Company with Artistic Director Lisa Steindler and Magic Theatre with Managing Director David Jobin. Directed by Kate Warner.

Stage Manager . . . . .Angela Nostrand
Scenic Design . . . . Erik Flatmo
Lighting Design . . . . .Jarrod Fischer
Sound Design . . . . .Sara Huddleston
Costumes Design . . . . .Alexae Visel

With the following cast:
KEVIN . . . . Eric Kerr
BLAKE . . . . .Patrick Alparone
MAX . . . . Liam Vincent
ANDY . . . . Brad Erickson
TELEGRAM DELIVERY BOY . . . . .Rowan Brooks

LIST OF PLAYERS

KEVIN – A man, 20s, handsome, bright, rational, arrogant, reckless

BLAKE – A man, 20s, witty, innocence and care, maybe a bit hipster

MAX – A man, 30s, all charm and somewhat like a predatory cat

ANDY – A man, 40s, fit, confident, aging well and suspending disbelief

TELEGRAM DELIVERY BOY – A younger man, an idea of youth, beauty and vitality all wrapped in a tight, snappy outfit. A slice of Americana, but there is something darker underneath.

NOTES

[ ] indicate overlapping dialogue.

The play should be performed without an intermission.

The ROAR is the sound of a huge beast trapped underwater, the sounds of an immense, graceful undersea animal twisted into something ferocious and ravenous. Somehow muted, dense and distant, except for scene 5 when it achieves deafening levels.

1

*(Waves of blue light illuminate a small apartment. An area stage right is in darkness. A sunken living room sits down stage center with a couch, a chair and a small table. There are French doors stage right that lead to an unseen kitchen. Two steps lead up to a front door stage left. A bedroom area is upstage center, raised higher. The bed is central, sitting in front of looming factory windows. **BLAKE** leans against the couch staring at the front door, foot tapping. **KEVIN** enters with a wine bottle and two glasses, The blue light fades, interior light prevails…)*

BLAKE. When did you tell them to come?

*(Pause. **KEVIN** sets the wine and glasses down on the table.)*

Kevin, when did you tell them to be here?

KEVIN. 8:30.

BLAKE. Well it's 8:35.

KEVIN. By your watch.

*(**KEVIN** exits.)*

BLAKE. It's after 8:30. They're late.

KEVIN. *(Entering again with two more glasses and a bottle opener. He puts the corkscrew in and begins to try to remove the cork from the wine bottle.)* So?

BLAKE. So they're not here yet, they're late.

KEVIN. So?

BLAKE. Maybe they're not coming.

KEVIN. I'm pretty sure they're coming, Baby.

BLAKE. Maybe they decided to do something else.

KEVIN. Maybe they're gonna' hook up with some other couple?

BLAKE. You don't know.

KEVIN. They'll be here Blake, take it easy. Jesus, I can't get this cork out.

BLAKE. White wine?

KEVIN. It's a Riesling. Um…"Bishop."

BLAKE. I don't even know what that means.

KEVIN. It means it was cheap. It's a dessert wine, or, I don't know, something like that. It's sweet.

BLAKE. Nice. Dessert. I get it.

KEVIN. It's all we have and they were both drinking white wine at the bar the other night, okay?

BLAKE. I'm just a little nervous. Not just a little, [maybe…]

KEVIN. [You gotta'] take a breath or something, okay? We agreed [and…]

BLAKE. [I only] [agreed to…]

KEVIN. [Ah ah, we] agreed and it's gonna' be fun and it's gonna' be fine and you're gonna' be great so…

(He moves in close to **BLAKE** *and gives him a deliberate kiss.)*

Take a breath.

*(***KEVIN*** returns to trying to get the cork out of the bottle. Pause)*

BLAKE. I look okay?

KEVIN. You look amazing. You always look amazing.

BLAKE. You look good too.

KEVIN. I know.

BLAKE. I thought maybe I should wear khakis, but the jeans look better with this shirt and I didn't know if we were supposed to dress up, ya' know? What time did you tell them to come?

KEVIN. Blake, don't ask me that again.

(The cork suddenly pops out, surprising **KEVIN***. He hops back holding the wine away, spilling a bit. He licks it off his fingers.)*

Got it!

BLAKE. Can we not do this?

(pause)

KEVIN. I thought you wanted to do this, right, Baby?

BLAKE. You want to do this and I said [okay.]

KEVIN. [Wait a] minute, that's not [how…]

BLAKE. [I want to] do it if you want to do it, but I don't really want to, unless you really do.

KEVIN. Wait, what?

BLAKE. That made sense.

KEVIN. They seem like really nice guys, right? And they're good looking and they've been committed forever, so it's not gonna' get all 'fatal attraction' or whatever. And they're on the way here. They're practically here.

BLAKE. I know.

KEVIN. I mean they're practically here and you don't wanna' go through with it?

BLAKE. Look, I'm, I don't know.

KEVIN. Well that's gonna' be awkward.

BLAKE. It's going to be awkward either way Kevin, don't be all dreamy about it. I don't want to go through with it and have it fuck things up.

KEVIN. It's just for fun, it's exciting, it's not gonna' fuck anything up.

BLAKE. Right, you know because you've done this before?

KEVIN. No, because…there is no one I could love or enjoy more than you. This can't touch that, this is, this'll just be an excellent story one day.

BLAKE. That's sweet and just really adorable and stupid.

KEVIN. Hey!

BLAKE. Seriously, Andy and Max have been together for, like, ever; we haven't. There's a big difference there, you know? Those guys are more…established with each other.

KEVIN. They've got nothing on us.

BLAKE. Age and experience.

KEVIN. Here we go…

BLAKE. Look, okay, I know it's just, I know it's not technically a big deal. It's something fun for us and I do like [them…]

KEVIN. [And…?]

BLAKE. And I feel like we might not be ready to sleep with other guys.

KEVIN. Only one way to find out.

BLAKE. Stop trying to be cute.

KEVIN. You're just doing your freak out thing. I love you and I know you, better than probably anyone, right? You're just doing your thing. It's like when I wanted to get a puppy.

BLAKE. It is so not like that.

KEVIN. It's just like that. And so we didn't get a puppy, did we? No really cute Weimaraner puppy, no adorable Weimaraner puppy. Think about how happy we'd be coming home to a fun little Weimaraner, but look around and no Weimaraner to [be found.]

BLAKE. [Stop] saying Weimaraner. And this isn't a puppy.

KEVIN. That's right! It's better. We don't have to train them or feed them or walk them. We just get to fuck them and then they leave.

BLAKE. *(crashing onto the couch)* Oh God.

KEVIN. That's it. That's all it is. It's just sex.

BLAKE. You're not gonna' call it off are you?

KEVIN. Only if you really, really want me to call it off. If you really want me to, I'll tell these attractive, charming, probably really, huh, really good in bed guys to go home.

(**BLAKE** *smiles, then shakes it off…*)

BLAKE. Doesn't it say something about, I don't know, us? I don't want to be all, it just seems like a big thing to try.

KEVIN. Better that we try it together, right?

BLAKE. As opposed to what?

*(**KEVIN** is caught, he hands **BLAKE** a glass of wine.)*

KEVIN. I don't know, just…better that we try it together, right?

(pause)

Okay, okay look, what if, what if we come up with some kind of signal? Like if either one of us wants to call it off once they're here, so it won't be obvious and we can get out of it.

BLAKE. What kind of signal?

KEVIN. Like a word, something we don't usually say. And if things get scary or you start to feel uncomfortable, you can just say it and we'll stop.

BLAKE. No matter what?

KEVIN. No matter what.

BLAKE. Okay, all right, that sounds okay.

KEVIN. Good! Good, okay, what word? You pick the word.

BLAKE. I don't know, um…"Palomino."

KEVIN. Like…the horses?

BLAKE. Fine, you pick something.

KEVIN. No, no, no, "Palomino" is fine.

BLAKE. Good.

KEVIN. Good.

BLAKE. *(sipping the wine…)* Oh, it is sweet.

(There's a knock at the door.)

KEVIN. So whaddya' think?

BLAKE. And we can stop any [time?]

KEVIN. [Come on] baby, whaddya' want me to do?

(another knock at the door)

BLAKE. Okay. It's an adventure. I mean, they're here, we're here, let's do it.

KEVIN. Okay, okay?

BLAKE. Okay. I love you, Kevin.

KEVIN. *(**KEVIN** bounces back to **BLAKE**, gives him a kiss…)* I love you too, Baby.

(**KEVIN** *opens the door.* **ANDY** *and* **MAX** *are waiting. They are a photo from an upscale catalogue; casual dress but very nice and totally at ease.* **ANDY** *has a bottle of wine. They enter, hugging* **KEVIN**.)

ANDY. Listen, I know we're a little late, I wanted to pick up something to bring you guys and like a total dunce I waited 'til the [last minute.]

MAX. [Ah, ah,] he got something good though. Hey.

KEVIN. You didn't have to do that.

ANDY. It's only wine, I hope you like Pinot Grigio, I didn't know [if you…]

KEVIN. [That's great,] we love it.

BLAKE. Hey Andy. Hey Max.

MAX. You're looking good tonight, Blake.

BLAKE. Thanks.

(**ANDY** *notices the open bottle of wine.*)

ANDY. Good, I'm glad you guys already started.

KEVIN. He already had a whole bottle.

BLAKE. I did not.

KEVIN. We did, before this one. You know, to relax a little [and kinda'…]

BLAKE. [It's no big] deal.

MAX. No, no, it's our fault for being late. Sorry.

ANDY. (*Setting down his bottle and picking up the open one. He examines the label.*) You guys are roughing it, huh?

KEVIN. Huh?

MAX. Andy's a wine snob, just ignore him.

ANDY. I am not a snob, I just have…

(*pause*)

MAX. Yes? We're waiting, you have…?

ANDY. I enjoy specific tastes.

MAX. Ah, me too.

(an awkward silence)

BLAKE. I'm glad you could make it tonight, this is good, I think it's gonna' be good, right?

(Another silence. They all slowly begin to laugh at their own awkwardness.)

MAX. Listen guys, it's going to be fine. It's not a big deal.

KEVIN. That's what I was saying to Blake before you [got...]

BLAKE. [Kevin.]

ANDY. Max is just like that, everything's fine.

MAX. And it is.

ANDY. And I always get a little, you know...

BLAKE. Nervous?

ANDY. I don't know, something like that.

KEVIN. Why don't I put on some music?

MAX. Good plan.

KEVIN. I'm not sure what we have exactly...

(KEVIN crosses to the stereo and finds something to play.)

BLAKE. Do you do this a lot?

KEVIN. He doesn't [mean...]

BLAKE. [No, it's] just, we never talked about that I guess, at the bar, and I wanted to know. I feel like we, we kinda' talked around it, so...

MAX. Did we talk around it? I thought Kevin was pretty well [versed in...]

ANDY. [Blake, you] can ask us whatever you want.

BLAKE. So, okay, do you do this a lot?

MAX. We do it sometimes.

ANDY. Really, it used to be a lark, you know, seems like more [lately.]

MAX. [Now Andy,] they'll think [we...]

ANDY. [Now] whenever Max starts to feel [a little...]

MAX. [We do it] every once in a while. And it's never a big deal, is it? No. Everything's fine.

KEVIN. Right.

*(Soft music fills the space as **KEVIN** returns to the group. The sounds of Bjork's "Possibly, Maybe" or something like it.)*

MAX. Listen, here's the thing, it's something guys do. It's something people do. All the time. And I really hope it's something we're going to do. Tonight.

BLAKE. Okay…I need some more wine.

KEVIN. Got it.

*(Grabs the bottle from **ANDY**, pours more into **BLAKE**'s waiting glass. He then pours a glass for himself. He turns to **ANDY**…)*

Wine?

ANDY. Um…maybe I'll open this bottle?

MAX. I told you.

ANDY. I just, um, don't like Rieslings is all.

MAX. He loves Rieslings.

ANDY. Stop it.

BLAKE. Kevin thought a dessert wine would be kind of appropriate.

MAX. I get that.

ANDY. Can I just grab the bottle opener?

(He snaps it up, cracking into opening his bottle.)

KEVIN. I really am sorry, Andy, it's all we had.

MAX. I'll take a glass of yours, Kevin.

ANDY. Oh that's right, I'm the bad guy.

MAX. *(He rubs his hand through **BLAKE**'s hair…)* I just want the sweet one.

ANDY. Uh huh.

*(**ANDY** pops his bottle open and pours himself a glass.)*

Well I will proudly be the lone friend to this bottle.

(another silence, longer, furtive glances, darting eyes)

MAX. Jesus, we're so fucking awkward.

*(Everyone laughs weakly. **MAX** takes off his coat. He then pulls his shirt up over his head and throws it at **BLAKE**.)*

BLAKE. Um…

ANDY. Just leave him; he's in his element. Max is always the first person to get undressed at any occasion.

MAX. That's right. And proud of it.

ANDY. We're both proud.

*(**MAX** laughs. **BLAKE** holds **MAX**'s shirt and sets is to the side.)*

BLAKE. Definitely need to drink more.

KEVIN. Maybe you should finish that glass first, Baby?

BLAKE. Oh.

*(He drinks the glass of wine. **MAX** takes off his pants, standing in front of the men in briefs.)*

ANDY. And here we go.

MAX. All right, come on. We can drink wine in any attire. Come on. Kevin?

*(**KEVIN** gets up and begins taking off his clothes. **BLAKE** follows suit shortly. **MAX** "assists" **BLAKE**. They all watch each other. **ANDY** takes it in, eyes on **MAX** and sipping his wine.)*

MAX. Now we've got a party.

*(**KEVIN** reaches his underwear quickly. He stops.)*

KEVIN. Andy, are you gonna'…?

ANDY. Absolutely.

*(Pause. Like **BLAKE** before him, he drinks his entire glass of wine at once. He then gets up and begins to undress. **MAX** begins kissing **BLAKE** as he finishes undressing him down to nothing. **KEVIN** crosses over to **ANDY** and begins taking off **ANDY**'s clothes. They too begin to kiss. **MAX***

breaks from **BLAKE**, *now naked, and quickly strips off his own underwear, as* **BLAKE** *looks back at* **KEVIN**, *who is now kissing* **ANDY**. **MAX** *takes* **BLAKE** *in and grapples him into a deeper kiss.)*

(ANDY *breaks from* **KEVIN** *and leads him over to* **BLAKE** *and* **MAX**. **ANDY** *strips off his underwear and steps up behind them as* **BLAKE** *and* **MAX** *continue to embrace. He joins them. Just for a moment,* **KEVIN** *is left outside the scene, the only man still wearing something. He takes in the moment.)*

(BLAKE *breaks away from between* **MAX** *and* **ANDY** *and pulls* **KEVIN** *into the mix. He is quickly stripped of his underwear. The men consume each other, melding into one flesh.)*

(The music begins to rise with the intensity of the scene.)

(After a moment, **MAX** *breaks away, tugging* **BLAKE** *by the hand towards the bed.* **BLAKE** *in turn pulls* **ANDY** *by the hand and* **ANDY** *pulls* **KEVIN** *by the hand; a chain of men moving around the living room and up to the bed. One by one they fall into each other on the bed, becoming something else all together, a mix of bodies and roaming arms and hands as the lights fade to the wavy blues and then to dark.)*

End Scene

2

*(Waves of blue light again illuminate the apartment. All evidence of the gathering is gone. **BLAKE** is in bed, in his underwear, twisted up in the sheets. The blue light gives way to interior lighting in the apartment and sun floods in through the windows.)*

*(Keys are heard and **KEVIN** enters through the front door carrying groceries.)*

*(**BLAKE** rolls over. He sits up in bed, rubs his eyes.)*

BLAKE. Good morning.

KEVIN. It's 12:30.

BLAKE. 12:30?

*(**KEVIN** moves through the room without stopping to talk to **BLAKE**, crossing into the kitchen.)*

Do we have any tea?

(Pause. Then louder…)

Did you make tea this morning, is there any left?

KEVIN. *(crossing back into the room, but standing just inside the door)* What?

BLAKE. *(sleepy, sweet…)* Is there any tea?

KEVIN. It's 12:30.

BLAKE. It's Saturday.

KEVIN. It's 12:30.

BLAKE. Okay…?

KEVIN. So do you want me to make you tea, Blake?

BLAKE. What is wrong with you?

KEVIN. I'll make you some tea.

BLAKE. I'm serious, I…

(He disappears again into the kitchen.)

Listen…

(pause, then louder:)

Listen, I don't know what's wrong with you but I'm getting pretty sick of it. Did you hear me?

(**KEVIN** *reappears in the doorway. Pause.*)

BLAKE. *(continued)* I said that I'm getting [pretty...]

KEVIN. [I heard] you Blake. I was in there making some nice afternoon tea for you to help you get your day started and I could hear you just fine, Blake.

BLAKE. Stop saying my name like it doesn't taste good.

KEVIN. I'm not.

BLAKE. Like you have to spit it out.

KEVIN. Is that what I'm doing...Blake?

(**KEVIN** *disappears into the kitchen again.*)

BLAKE. Jesus, why are you being such an asshole? I know it's not because I slept late, I always sleep late on Saturday and you've been acting like this for weeks now. Ever since you orchestrated your little jamboree with the wine connoisseurs, and it wasn't even my idea, so I'm not [sure what the...]

(**KEVIN** *reappears suddenly.*)

KEVIN. [My little] jamboree?

BLAKE. Party, event, foursome, you pick.

KEVIN. Sure, I planned it, fine. But you were the star, right?

BLAKE. How can you be the star of group sex?

KEVIN. You don't know because you were the star.

BLAKE. And what, you weren't? Max was all over you.

KEVIN. I was all over Max.

BLAKE. Super.

KEVIN. No, I was on the outside.

BLAKE. Come on.

KEVIN. I was on the outside.

BLAKE. That's bed geography, that's not my fault; I was just going with the flow. I was just trying to have an adventure, right?

KEVIN. You sure did.

BLAKE. Fuck you. Fuck. You. It was your idea, I did it for you, so you could [feel like...]

KEVIN. [You may have] agreed to it for me, but you sure seemed to get into [it once…]

BLAKE. *(laughing in disbelief…)* [Um,] yeah! It's sex. It feels good.

KEVIN. Look, I'm making the fucking tea; do we need to talk about this now?

BLAKE. Yes. You don't get to stomp around here with your big judgment boots feeling like you've somehow been wronged when I was trying to call the thing off and I felt self-conscious and dumb when they showed up dressed nice and radiating 'couple-hood.'

KEVIN. *(stuck…)* Judgment boots?

BLAKE. That's what I said: judgment boots.

KEVIN. What the fuck is a judgment boot?

BLAKE. I didn't do anything to make you feel bad, Kevin, I wouldn't do that and I don't want you to be mad at me so stop it.

KEVIN. It was supposed to be our adventure, Baby.

BLAKE. Right, our adventure?

KEVIN. Turned out as your adventure.

BLAKE. Is that what it was?

(He gets up out of the bed.)

Because it's not the one I would have picked.

(He grabs the comforter off the bed and wraps it around himself.)

I would have picked white water rafting, or skydiving… no, that's a lie. That's a lie. I'm just trying to sound rugged. I would have picked Disneyland for an adventure. That Mad Hatter thing, the spinning teacups, that's about my speed. And you know it. You know it. Not sex with some other guys we just met at a local bar.

*(**KEVIN** softens…)*

KEVIN. We didn't just meet them.

BLAKE. I can't believe I was so, I mean, those guys could've been anyone.

KEVIN. That was supposed to be the exciting part. Or something like that.

BLAKE. That was the exciting part?

KEVIN. Or something like that.

BLAKE. Spinning teacups, Kevin. Go fuck yourself.

*(He passes **KEVIN** on the way into the kitchen; still wrapped in the comforter. **KEVIN** goes to the bed and examines it.)*

KEVIN. I think I'm gonna' wash the sheets again.

(He straightens the pillows and fixes the sheet a little. Then to the bed, to himself…)

Stupid sheets.

*(**BLAKE** comes back in with two mugs. He sets one down on the end table and takes the other with him to sit in the chair, the comforter around him.)*

Is that mine?

BLAKE. If you want it I guess.

KEVIN. Thanks.

BLAKE. You pretty much made it.

*(**KEVIN** sits on the couch. They both pout a little.)*

KEVIN. Well this doesn't feel very good.

BLAKE. Nope.

KEVIN. So…

BLAKE. So stop being angry at me. On a Saturday.

KEVIN. I know.

BLAKE. I know you know. And unless you want me to break out the Sigur Rós albums, you better start being nice again.

KEVIN. *(with a smile)* You can't threaten me.

BLAKE. Electric strings and sky-high vocals.

KEVIN. I'm not afraid.

BLAKE. I will go over there right now and put on a bootleg, all B-sides EP of the most experimental [music.]

KEVIN. [Okay you] win. I don't know, Baby, it just wasn't what I thought is all. I thought it would be all sexy and feel good and, I don't know, but the whole time it just felt weird. And then, after a while, I kinda' became aware that I wasn't even touching you.

BLAKE. Well I mean, what did you expect?

(Pause. He puts his hand on **KEVIN***'s leg…)*

You wanted other guys, so other guys were here. Not me, other guys. With fancy wine.

(There is a knock at the door.)

KEVIN. Are you expecting anyone?

BLAKE. *(He pulls the blanket up around his head.)* I'm wearing a comforter.

KEVIN. It looks like a parka.

BLAKE. It doesn't look like a parka.

KEVIN. Like a little Eskimo.

*(***KEVIN*** kisses* **BLAKE***. Another knock.)*

BLAKE. Ugh, I'm not expecting anyone.

*(***KEVIN*** goes to the door, opens it. In the doorway stands a bright, young* **TELEGRAM DELIVERY BOY** *in a form-fitting shirt and pants; shades of blue and a matching hat. He is soaking wet, entirely, water visibly dripping from him. He holds a yellow envelope.)*

TELEGRAM DELIVERY BOY. Good afternoon sir.

KEVIN. Um…

TELEGRAM DELIVERY BOY. I have a telegram for Mr. Blake Fields.

KEVIN. A telegram?

BLAKE. I'm Blake.

TELEGRAM DELIVERY BOY. Then this is for you.

KEVIN. You're soaking wet.

TELEGRAM DELIVERY BOY. Yes. Oh, I mean, darn this crazy weather. Never can tell what's coming.

(He hands **BLAKE** *the yellow envelope. The ROAR sounds from far away, the* **TELEGRAM DELIVERY BOY** *looks over his shoulder.)*

KEVIN. What the hell was that?

TELEGRAM DELIVERY BOY. Thunder?

BLAKE. It didn't sound like thunder?

TELEGRAM DELIVERY BOY. Have a nice day sir.

(He exits with a smile, whistling a little tune.)

KEVIN. It was clear, was there like a flash shower or something?

(He looks up at the sky then closes the door as **BLAKE** *crosses to the couch.)*

BLAKE. I didn't even know you could still send telegrams.

KEVIN. Mostly for money orders and stuff I think.

BLAKE. Money? Nice.

(He opens the envelope and pulls out the carbon paper telegram. He reads:)

8:08 AM "We regret to inform you that [Andy] has gone to live at the bottom of the ocean. Stop. Please accept his deepest apologies, but he will no longer be in contact. Stop. Should you wish to see him, you unfortunately cannot. Stop."

(Pause. He looks up…)

KEVIN. So…it's from Andy?

BLAKE. It's about Andy anyway.

KEVIN. And that's it?

BLAKE. That's it.

KEVIN. There's got to be more.

BLAKE. *(***BLAKE** *checks the back of the telegram with a shrug.)* Nope.

KEVIN. Why is Andy sending you a telegram?

BLAKE. It doesn't say who it's from.

KEVIN. Well maybe Andy was impressed, maybe he thinks you're pretty [special?]

BLAKE. [Oh, don't] start again with the stupid jealousy [stuff.]

KEVIN. [Well why] is Andy sending you little messages?

BLAKE. Okay, does this sound like a love note to you?

KEVIN. Not exactly.

BLAKE. No. No, it doesn't.

KEVIN. Fine. I'm sorry.

BLAKE. I really wish you could hear what you sound like when you say that. I don't think it comes out the way you think it does. Good thing I'm so patient.

KEVIN. In your cute little comforter.

BLAKE. Alright, okay, I'm getting dressed.

(He rises, pulling the comforter up around himself again. **KEVIN** *grabs the edge of the comforter and pulls it off of* **BLAKE** *as he walks away.)*

KEVIN. I kinda' like this look.

BLAKE. Uh huh. Make the bed.

*(***BLAKE*** exits towards the kitchen. ***KEVIN*** picks up the telegram and calls after him.)*

KEVIN. For a minute, I really thought it might be money.

BLAKE. *(from off)* What?

KEVIN. Nothing.

(Examining the telegram. To himself…)

I'm sure we'll figure it out.

End Scene

3

(Lights rise on the darkened stage right area to reveal **MAX** *waiting, drinking coffee from a paper to-go cup. He stares into the cup.)*

(The sounds of a crowded coffee shop fill the space.)

*(***KEVIN** *enters the stage with his own paper cup. He spots* **MAX** *and heads over towards him.)*

KEVIN. There you are.

MAX. *(startled from his thoughts, but quick to put on a show…)* Here I am.

KEVIN. I didn't even know this little corner was back here.

MAX. I should have been on the look out. My head is kinda' all over the place. So what's up, I was surprised to hear from you actually?

KEVIN. I've been leaving you messages for over [a week.]

MAX. [Because I] haven't seen you at the bar, in a while?

KEVIN. Oh…you know, things have just been kinda' crazy the past couple weeks, haven't been going out much.

MAX. Uh huh.

KEVIN. And Blake has been really irritable lately, so going out [has been…]

MAX. [We're] all adults, I know how it works. No excuses, you're off the hook.

KEVIN. But I'm [not…]

MAX. [You] said it was important?

KEVIN. Okay, okay I called you because we got, no, Blake got this, I don't know what to call it, weird? I keep calling it weird, this weird message delivered by some guy. I don't know if it's "important" exactly. He just showed up at the door, soaking wet and said [something…]

MAX. [Wet?]

KEVIN. Yep. Strange, right?

MAX. Strange.

KEVIN. Well I know I was kinda' cryptic on the phone, but it is kind of…

MAX. Weird.

KEVIN. Sure. And I just wanted to see if you guys could shed some light on it, but you sounded [so…]

MAX. [It's just] a little rough right now is all.

KEVIN. What's that?

MAX. Well I'm glad you called, I needed to get out of the house anyway. There's some kind of, some kind of problem with the pipes. Water everywhere, it's ridiculous, can't figure out where it's coming from. We just refinished the floors and they're ruined. Everything's ruined.

KEVIN. That's awful.

MAX. What?

KEVIN. That's awful, about the water.

MAX. Oh yes, no, it'll be fine. It's fine, it's nothing…I like it more here anyway.

KEVIN. The coffee shop?

MAX. Well not necessarily this coffee shop; you don't like this place?

KEVIN. No, I like it. It's really…rustic.

MAX. Huh.

KEVIN. Or I don't know, but it's nice.

MAX. No, it is sort of warm and rustic.

KEVIN. I think Blake would like it; he's drawn to anything remotely pastoral and these paintings [are just…]

MAX. [Well it's] not, it doesn't have to be this place in particular, just in public, around people.

KEVIN. Are you all right?

MAX. Sure, absolutely.

KEVIN. Okay.

MAX. I just feel better around people right now.

KEVIN. What's going on Max?

MAX. Nothing. Nothing. You look good. When you guys stopped coming to the, when you "got busy," I kinda' thought I wouldn't see you again, but here you are.

(MAX *touches* KEVIN*'s hands, but* KEVIN *pulls them away with a self-conscious grin.*)

Oh…you already ordered, okay, what'd you get? I always get a black coffee. That's it, nothing extra, but Andy always got some thing that took ten minutes to order and had six kinds of whip cream and nonsense on top, you've seen those, with the foam and syrup and all the layers, like some kind of insane, caffeinated yard sale in a cup, he said it was a texture thing but, I mean, Jesus it's just fucking coffee.

KEVIN. Um…right.

MAX. So Andy and I broke up.

KEVIN. What?

MAX. I broke up with Andy actually, it doesn't feel like that, but that's what happened. I left him, or I told him to leave.

KEVIN. But you guys were together [for so…]

MAX. [Well] nothing lasts forever and all that other stuff you're supposed to say. But we just decided, I decided that I, you never really know how you're gonna' react to things, you know?

KEVIN. I don't know, like what?

MAX. Oh you know, he's just…Andy has very specific ideas about what "things" mean. Actually mean. Everything means something; everything's so serious. Frankly, he's always been older on the inside, even before he started actually getting older. You know what I mean, right?

KEVIN. I kinda' thought you guys were about the same age?

(Pause. **MAX** *takes long look at* **KEVIN**, *takes a breath, but then drinks his coffee instead of speaking.)*

MAX. You needed something, wanted to ask, right, about this wet guy leaving a message for you?

KEVIN. Well, okay, this is a little touchier now, but it's about Andy actually; I was hoping you could help [explain it.]

MAX. [What] about Andy?

KEVIN. I think maybe it's from Andy. Something about the ocean [and…?]

MAX. [What do you,] what kind of message?

KEVIN. Believe it or not, it's a telegram.

(Producing the telegram, KEVIN *hands it to* MAX. MAX *takes the telegram hesitantly, as if it might hurt him to touch it.* MAX *reads the telegram out loud.)*

MAX. 8:08 AM "We regret to inform you that [Andy] has gone to live at the bottom of the ocean. Stop.

*(*MAX *trails off, reading the telegram to himself.)*

KEVIN. So we really didn't know what to make of it. And it seemed kinda' off to me that Andy would be sending Blake messages.

MAX. Off?

KEVIN. That Andy would be sending something to Blake.

MAX. Doesn't look like it's from him.

KEVIN. Who else would have [sent it?]

MAX. [I got] one like this; no, not like this. But I got a telegram. I guess the guy was wet now that I think about it, I guess I didn't notice, I just, I can't believe you got this.

KEVIN. Well can we ask Andy?

(Pause. MAX *is transfixed by the telegram.)*

Max?

MAX. What?

KEVIN. I know you guys, look I know it's not the best timing and maybe you're not on the best of terms right now, but this is bizarre right? This is not a normal thing. So can we ask him?

MAX. What's wrong with you?

KEVIN. What do you [mean?]

MAX. [What's] wrong with you?

KEVIN. Nothing.

MAX. I can't ask him. Ask him? Did you read this, you fucking little kid; did you read this? How the fuck am I supposed to ask him if he's at the bottom of the God damn ocean?!

KEVIN. Jesus, calm [down.]

MAX. [How am] I supposed to ask him [anything?]

KEVIN. [Look, I] didn't mean [to...]

MAX. [You didn't.]

KEVIN. Keep your voice down man, [people are...]

MAX. [Fuck!]

> (*pause*)

> Fuck, I shouldn't have...lost my temper. Fuck. I'm sorry.

KEVIN. It's, just, it's okay.

MAX. I hate when I get all...ugh, it's just awkward. It's not...

> (*Pause.* **MAX** *tries to pull himself together.*)

> What, what kind of coffee did you get?

KEVIN. It's, um...it's tea.

MAX. Tea.

KEVIN. Green tea. We, um, don't really do coffee.

MAX. (*Laughing to himself, a bitter sound...*) Perfect.

KEVIN. It makes us both jittery.

MAX. Listen, I don't know why you got that telegram. If I knew, I'd...tell you. Are we done now, can we be done?

KEVIN. If you hear from him [will you...]

MAX. [If I hear] from him.

KEVIN. All right. Sorry if I...just, sorry.

> (**KEVIN** *awkwardly begins to hug* **MAX**, *then decides against it and begins to exit. He gets half way across the stage as* **MAX** *recovers, putting his charmer routine back on...*)

MAX. Kevin. Kevin, come back for a second. Please?

> (**KEVIN** *turns and crosses back to* **MAX**.)

KEVIN. Uh huh?

MAX. Look, I know I'm kinda' all over the place right now.

KEVIN. I understand man.

MAX. No. No. I think you and Blake are great and I don't want you to think that Andy and I just do that kind of thing all the time. I mean we do that kind of thing, did that kind of thing, but not all the time. So don't think [we're…]

KEVIN. [Oh, I] didn't [think that.]

MAX. [Andy's sick,] he's sick.

KEVIN. I don't [understand.]

MAX. [We get, ya'] know, tested pretty regularly, it's never a big…it was never a big deal. He just got the results, right after, well after that night with you guys. Needless to say it was unexpected.

KEVIN. He got [the…?]

MAX. [So you] should get tested. There were all kinds of things we, I mean, it was a good night, but you guys should get tested.

KEVIN. He's sick?

MAX. Well, I mean, not "sick," not yet anyway, look, I'm sure it's nothing for you to…well, that's a stupid thing to say. I'm sure you're fine. Just to be safe. And whatever the other thing is…conscientious. But I thought I should tell you. Or, no, I decided to tell you. Just now.

KEVIN. Okay.

MAX. I'm sure you guys are fine. I'm not sure, but we were pretty safe.

KEVIN. Pretty safe.

MAX. You know, nothing's for sure. I should get going.

KEVIN. How's, I mean, how is Andy doing with…all this?

MAX. I don't know Kevin. He's at the bottom of the fucking ocean.

(**MAX** *exits.*)

(**KEVIN** *stand with his cup, unable to move. He drops the cup, spilling his tea on the floor. This jars him out of his thoughts, the liquid splashing on his feet snapping him back into the moment.*)

End Scene

4

*(Waves of blue lights again illuminate the apartment.
BLAKE enters and sits on the couch with a bowl of cereal.
He is in pajama bottoms and a t-shirt. The blue light
gives way to interior lighting in the apartment as **KEVIN**
enters…)*

BLAKE. Where've you been?

KEVIN. I got coffee.

BLAKE. Coffee?

KEVIN. Tea.

BLAKE. You've been gone forever.

KEVIN. I had some other, had some errands.

BLAKE. Want some cereal?

KEVIN. No.

BLAKE. Are you sure? It's Captain Crunch…fresh from the
ocean floor.

> *(He laughs at his own joke. **KEVIN** does not. They share
> a look…)*

Oh come on, that was funny.

KEVIN. It wasn't funny, okay?

BLAKE. No really, I've been thinking about this: how the
fuck does someone go to the ocean floor? Unless they
have one of those mini-subs, like in that documentary
we saw, but I doubt that's what's going on and if it's
not just a lame prank then maybe Andy's crazy, like
one of those weirdo guys that [can't let…]

KEVIN. [Shut-up.]

BLAKE. Um, ouch.

KEVIN. Sorry.

BLAKE. You're letting this telegram thing get to you too
much. It's just some kind of joke.

KEVIN. I don't know.

BLAKE. Okay smarty pants, what is it then?

KEVIN. Andy tested positive.

BLAKE. Positive for what?

KEVIN. *(dumbfounded)* What?

BLAKE. What?

KEVIN. What do you, he tested positive. Positive.

BLAKE. What!! How did, how do you know!

KEVIN. Max told me, I met him for coffee and he just blurted [it out…]

BLAKE. [You met] Max for coffee?

KEVIN. I went to ask him about the telegram.

BLAKE. Who cares about the fucking…

(*Pause.* **KEVIN** *sits down next to him…*)

Jesus.

KEVIN. I know.

BLAKE. Was Max, how was Max?

KEVIN. Strange.

BLAKE. Did he, I mean, I don't even know.

KEVIN. It's still kinda' sinking in I think. And they broke up.

BLAKE. Jesus… bad week.

KEVIN. Uh, yeah, bad week.

BLAKE. Well I don't know, should we maybe…

(**BLAKE** *stops, something washes over him.*)

KEVIN. What is it?

BLAKE. I'm so, I almost said, "Should we send him a card?"

KEVIN. I don't think they make cards for that.

BLAKE. Maybe it's a, this is so bizarre; he didn't look sick. Did he?

KEVIN. Oh Blake, that's the stupidest fucking [thing to…]

BLAKE. [Well I've] never even known anyone who had it, so I'm sorry if I don't know how it's supposed to look.

KEVIN. Of course you've known people who've, what are you talking about? You know people who have it now.

BLAKE. No I don't. Who?

KEVIN. Lots of, Dan that was at Thanksgiving with us last year. Toby, the bartender you flirt with at the bar all [the time.]

BLAKE. [Toby?]

KEVIN. You just don't know they have it. There's no big flashing sign or [anything.]

BLAKE. [Of course] there's no, come on, it's just; he didn't "look" sick.

KEVIN. It doesn't look like anything, what's wrong [with you?]

BLAKE. [It's just the first] thing that popped into my head, okay, give me a second to try and get my [brain into...]

KEVIN. [For fuck's] sake, did you not have, like, a 7th grade health class? How can you not know [these things?]

BLAKE. [A 7th grade] health class where we talked about this?

KEVIN. Yes!

BLAKE. No.

KEVIN. Well I did, and even if I didn't, there's a certain level of, I don't know, awareness that's, like, just out there, [right? That you pick up from...]

BLAKE. [Awareness is all there is.] There's so much fucking awareness, I mean, it's not even something people get anymore.

KEVIN. Apparently they do, [Blake.]

BLAKE. [Well] congratulations, you're right.

KEVIN. That's not even the point!

BLAKE. *(catching himself, something hard in the chest...)* We could have it. The point is, is we could have it.

> *(pause)*

KEVIN. We were safe and it shouldn't [be a...]

BLAKE. [We were] safe?

KEVIN. With Andy and Max.

> *(pause)*

KEVIN. *(continued)* We were safe, right?

    (Pause. BLAKE sits on the couch. KEVIN circles in behind him.)

    Blake?

    (pause)

BLAKE. I don't know.

KEVIN. What?

BLAKE. It got so, it just got [so…]

KEVIN. [Got so] what?

    (pause)

    What?

BLAKE. You were there, it was really intense and it happened really fast, once it started happening, all of it, and I think it started out safe, with Max, and then with Andy, I don't know, I want to know, just close my eyes and be sure, but I got, caught up, you know what I'm talking about. It's like a head rush; and everything, with all that going on, I don't even know if I would know the difference, everything gets so slippery, I just, I just got…

KEVIN. Excited.

BLAKE. Excited. So I don't know.

    (KEVIN sits down again next to BLAKE on the couch.)

KEVIN. I don't even; we've only ever had safe sex with each other. All this time. We've never messed that up, so [it's hard…]

BLAKE. [I've only] ever had safe sex ever.

KEVIN. Then how do you not know what you did with Andy?

BLAKE. Well that was new, okay? He was behind me and Max was in front of me on his knees [and…]

KEVIN. [Ugh, I don't] need the logistics.

BLAKE. You don't need the, it sounds like that's what we need to talk about. Were you safe, in all that?

KEVIN. Yes.

BLAKE. And what were your 'logistics?'

KEVIN. I said I don't want to talk [about it.]

BLAKE. [You wanna'] talk about me, what I did, but not "it." Fuck that. You know, ever since you said that thing to me the other day, that thing about how you realized you weren't touching me, I've been trying to figure out how that worked. Because I don't remember touching you either; I don't remember you in that situation. At all. And I can so clearly place Max and Andy in every configuration. Max kissing the back of my neck, Andy holding me, feeling me, his hands on the inside of my thigh, the feeling of Max inside [me…]

KEVIN. [Blake.]

BLAKE. […and where] my mouth was, where their mouths were, how they each tasted, different, Max tasted like cigarettes and Andy tasted like mint. And I remember you saying something at one point? But I don't remember you. That's strange, [isn't it?]

KEVIN. [You were] just drunk baby, now stop it, you're [just upset.]

BLAKE. [No, I was] tipsy and uncomfortable and excited and disoriented and, I was all kinds of things, but I wasn't so drunk that I don't know [you were…]

KEVIN. [I said] I don't want [to talk…]

BLAKE. [And yet, I] think we need to talk about the logistics, your logistics.

KEVIN. You can recall a lot for someone who can't remember.

BLAKE. Well do you remember if he wore anything? I'm sure you had a great view.

KEVIN. You're not even making sense.

BLAKE. No, I think [that you…]

KEVIN. [Stop it] [Blake.]

BLAKE. [I think] that I had sex with two guys that you wanted us both to have sex with while you watched from the edge of the bed.

KEVIN. I didn't just watch from the [edge of...]

BLAKE. [No, no I] gave you credit; you said something. And you sounded really far away. I could hear both of them breathing, feel one's breath in this ear, one in this ear, and you from somewhere. You remember what you said?

KEVIN. It was strange and [I didn't...]

BLAKE. [You] said: "That's good."

KEVIN. I just...

BLAKE. "That's good." Like a show, like some [kind of...]

KEVIN. [No, in the] middle of it, I just kinda' sat back and didn't know how to get back into it, just, I didn't know what to do.

BLAKE. Well, neither did I. And look at us now.

KEVIN. Now we...

(regrouping)

Now okay, so it might not show up yet, I don't know how it, I mean, I do know, it takes time, but it's been, we need to get tested to be sure.

BLAKE. I think I'm gonna' get some more cereal.

KEVIN. Blake.

BLAKE. I'm getting cereal.

KEVIN. Fuck that, we need to [get tested.]

BLAKE. [Right now?] Right this minute? Well let me just throw on some jeans and a scarf and we'll be out the door, fuck you. We don't need to do anything, you want me to get tested; I'm the one, right? Because it couldn't be you, could it? Because you somehow didn't know what to do?

(pause)

KEVIN. It wasn't supposed to be like that. When I imagined it, when I, when we planned it, it wasn't supposed [to be...]

BLAKE. [Did Max] and Andy break up, or did Max break

up with Andy?

KEVIN. I don't know. No, Max left Andy.

BLAKE. And where is Andy now?

KEVIN. I don't know [baby.]

BLAKE. [At the] bottom of the ocean?

KEVIN. No, that's [not...]

BLAKE. [But he's] not with Max.

(*pause*)

How long were they together?

(*pause*)

I'm out of cereal and I'm still hungry.

KEVIN. What if [you...]

BLAKE. [Lucky] charms, you think? I think I'll switch to Lucky Charms.

(**BLAKE** *begins to exit, then spins on his heel.*)

Ya' know, here's something I wanna' ask, just out of the blue maybe, before I enjoy some more cereal: do you love me?

KEVIN. (**KEVIN** *starts to speak, then stops.*) I love you.

BLAKE. It sounds funny.

KEVIN. Don't do that. Come on, Baby, we need to know, something bad might have happened.

BLAKE. You really don't get it. You feel that, that feeling right now? Something bad happened either way.

End Scene

5

(8,000 meters below the ocean's surface. A shaft of blue light cuts through the space revealing **ANDY**. *He is curled up on a small platform suspended above the playing area. Soaking wet, he wears only a pair of torn pants and he clutches a 19th Century whaling harpoon, almost as large as he is, close to his body. The harpoon is rusted, bound with fragments of thick rope and is terrifying in its size, something for fighting monsters.)*

ANDY. At the bottom of the ocean, in the deepest parts, so far down that even the muscular light from above can't push through the thick darkness, there's a quiet place. A very quiet, very still place. A place thick with resistance, that holds with a gentle grip, gentle but firm. Reassuring. Definitive. Isolated. So far away from anything of the every day world that everything up above just sinks to the back of the mind, becomes a story, a fairy tale that hangs on the edges of awareness. But it can no longer be seen, not in a real sense, and so it drifts away. Everything drifts away, lost in the gentle rhythms of the water moving around you, coaxing you and holding you all at once, like dancing in place.

(He rocks a bit with the harpoon, almost a little dance.)

With nothing but the rhythms of the current to feel, you begin to sense every little movement, even the smallest fish, some tiny, exotic thing never before imagined, all fins and tail; when it moves, you can feel it. The water carries an echo of the movement right to your skin. And when something bigger moves…you feel that too; the water pushing harder against you. And when something unimaginably large moves, you feel things that only someone alone on the ocean floor should ever feel. Because you can't imagine the unimaginable, you're never prepared for something so vast. Sitting at home, warm and familiar in a world full of daylight, no matter how confusing or difficult, it's still…safe. Safe in a way that's become second nature, common, even overlooked. And safe in a way that's assumed and expected and generally understood...

So it's a slippery kind of thing at best.

And the safer we are, the longer we're safe, the further away the horrors. Until it doesn't seem real anymore, until it becomes almost mythical, this fantastically destructive beast that couldn't really exist. Because how could anything so much more powerful than...

(The ROAR happens, deafeningly loud and closer than ever. It shakes the stage. **ANDY** *cowers, head down, clinging to the harpoon. A giant shadow passes over him in shapes, something moving above him. When the light returns, he is looking up, eyes struck wide with shock.)*

And now, face to face with it, so much larger than I could have imagined; so much more real. I'm awed by the very sight; the immediacy of its purpose, I know it, I can see it. And even if I could stave it off, I don't pretend that's enough, there is a, is a design to that kind of devastation, nowhere, nowhere has anyone bested this beast. And only in its presence can someone know how very large the ocean must be to hold such a monster. How very small we can be in its' wake.

And it's hard to wait alone. When the one thing that connects you most intimately to others, that feels so good, is the one thing...

(Pause. Then quickly, uncontrolled...)

To have someone, to be had by someone, that's so, amazing, it's the only thing that I ever, but no, no, it's so fleeting and fucking slick in my grasp, I couldn't keep a grip on it, especially when I needed it to be there, needed it more than anything and depending on it, depending on his, depending on someone else's heart, even a fool wouldn't...

(Pause. He puts his head in his hands, arms wrapped around the harpoon, holding it to his chest.)

Sometimes it's, I think I can still hear voices, people I

knew, people I cared about, from up above. They sound like whispers, muted; they make a sound like aching. I think if I tried, I could make it sharper, hear more. But I don't want to think that. I don't want to hear that. I don't want to hear anything that would make me want to go back. Tempt me. So I don't.

(As he continues, he slowly stands, using the harpoon as a crutch.)

At the bottom, you try to remember that it was hard for the people around you in a way that's not impossible to understand, but still agonizingly impossible to understand.

And so you leave daylight behind and let yourself sink down as far as you can, to the very bottom, where there's nothing but what's left to live. You make it easier; like a piece of candy, a morsel of bait, you offer yourself over… and you are wrecked. And you are taken. And you are…

*(Again the ROAR, the shadow moving across him as he looks up. The shadow passes and **ANDY** is gone.)*

End Scene

6

(800 meters above the ocean surface. Waves of blue light illuminate the apartment.)

(The blue light gives way to interior lighting in the apartment as a knock sounds at the door.)

(BLAKE *and* **KEVIN** *enter mid-argument, heading for the door...)*

BLAKE. The fact that you could say "over-reacting" to me is kind of [fucked up.]

KEVIN. [Okay, no,] you're not over-reacting to the, I mean, you're just over-reacting to my reaction.

BLAKE. One night on the couch wasn't enough for you?

KEVIN. It was plenty, that's why I'm trying to get [you to...]

BLAKE. [Have I cried?] Have I fallen apart? Have I punched you in the face for suggesting that you know how I should be acting?

(The knocking again. To the door...)

Hold on a second.

KEVIN. You haven't done anything like that [at all.]

BLAKE. [Well] maybe I'll try the punching thing, you [think?]

KEVIN. [Good. That] would be something. That's what I'm, listen, I think the way you're under-reacting is an over-reaction.

*(**BLAKE** pauses with his hand on the doorknob.)*

BLAKE. Stop and listen to yourself.

*(**BLAKE** opens the door. The* **TELEGRAM DELIVERY BOY** *stands there looking snappy, bright, soaking wet.)*

KEVIN. Oh Jesus...

TELEGRAM DELIVERY BOY. Good morning sir.

KEVIN. What's so good about it?

TELEGRAM DELIVERY BOY. It's a beautiful day outside.

KEVIN. Then why are you soaking wet?

TELEGRAM DELIVERY BOY. *(producing a telegram)* Yes sir, a beautiful day.

KEVIN. More fucking good news?

TELEGRAM DELIVERY BOY. I have a telegram for Mr. Blake Fields.

KEVIN. I'll take it.

TELEGRAM DELIVERY BOY. Oh, jeez, I'm sorry sir. I have to deliver it to Mr. Fields directly.

BLAKE. Got it.

*(**BLAKE** snaps the telegram from the **TELEGRAM DELIVERY BOY**s hand.)*

TELEGRAM DELIVERY BOY. Also a telegram for Mr. Blake Fields and Mr. Kevin Richards.

KEVIN. All right, that one I can take.

TELEGRAM DELIVERY BOY. Yes you can, sir.

(He hands over the telegram.)

KEVIN. And maybe you can explain a couple [of things…]

TELEGRAM DELIVERY BOY. [Gosh would] you look at the time. So many deliveries to make, I'll be off then. You gentlemen…

*(He stops. He reaches out and puts his hand on **BLAKE**'s shoulder in a supportive manner.)*

You have a nice day sir.

*(He exits, whistling a little tune. **BLAKE** closes the door.)*

BLAKE. That [was…]

KEVIN. [I think] next time we should call the cops.

BLAKE. Jesus, Kevin, he's just delivering telegrams.

KEVIN. Soaking wet from the bottom of the ocean?

*(Ignoring **KEVIN**, **BLAKE** tears into the first telegram.)*

BLAKE. 8:08 PM "We regret to inform you that, despite our best efforts, [Andy] has been killed by a sea monster at the bottom of the ocean. Stop. Please accept our deepest regrets, but he is in a better place. Stop. And he is no longer alone. Stop."

KEVIN. What the fuck?

BLAKE. I wonder what kind?

KEVIN. Huh?

BLAKE. What kind of sea monster? It doesn't say. They should tell us what kind of sea monster. It makes it worse if you have to imagine it.

KEVIN. (**KEVIN** *crushes the telegram into a ball and throws it away.*) It's fucking ridiculous.

BLAKE. I think I get it Kevin, it's supposed to be ridiculous.

KEVIN. Oh please, how do you get killed by a sea monster? If Andy was any kind of killed, we would hear about it from Max, not from zippy the shiny telegram guy.

(**KEVIN** *opens his telegram and reads it to himself.*)

BLAKE. What does it say?

KEVIN. 8:00 PM "[Andy] is sorry he didn't know. Stop. He didn't know to stop. Stop."
Fuck.

BLAKE. I wonder if I should feel it inside me, I'd think you could feel it on some really, really small level?

KEVIN. Stop it.

BLAKE. He didn't know to stop.

KEVIN. No. No, this doesn't mean anything. The ocean and sea monsters and all this morbid bullshit, it's just some stupid, I don't know, but it doesn't mean anything.

BLAKE. You should be able to tell if something's in you, it should give you that much.

KEVIN. Look, telegrams, stupid telegrams, are not how you figure out if, no, it's like I said, you'll just, you'll get a test and then we'll know. We'll both get a test.

BLAKE. I don't want to know.

KEVIN. You have to know.

BLAKE. No, I know how it sounds, but I really don't want to [know.]

KEVIN. [But not] knowing is worse [than...]

BLAKE. [Is it?] At least now there's still, still, I don't know, a chance [that…]

(**KEVIN** *mashes the telegram up into a ball.*)

KEVIN. [Blake] don't. Look, you're getting caught up in, whatever [this is, and…]

BLAKE. [We are] caught up in whatever [this is…]

KEVIN. [You gotta'] snap out of it, it's not real, [none of…]

BLAKE. [How do] you [know?]

KEVIN. [We need] to talk about, okay, we both have to try and figure out what's going on, I mean here in the real world, because I'm not one of those guys that is good with, I [mean, I don't…]

BLAKE. [This is the] real world, this [right here.]

KEVIN. [Quit, it, I'm] trying to talk [to you…]

BLAKE. [Stop "trying"] and just say [whatever you're…]

KEVIN. [It's not] okay.

BLAKE. I know it's [not okay.]

KEVIN. [It's not okay!] We don't know anything for sure. I don't know if you're okay, I mean even if you're not, I know there are pills now and all kinds of amazing, but that's not the, that doesn't make you not, on the inside you'd still, no, I try not to think about it, but I keep involuntarily running the possible outcomes through my head: what if this, what if that, but not in a good way, over and over, like every time I stop thinking about something specific, even for a second, my brain just automatically starts forecasting possible futures, for us, for me, for me, possibility after possibility, like noise, a flurry of, like little cuts from a movie. And some of them are, are, [are…]

BLAKE. [Are what?]

KEVIN. No, I, [I just..]

BLAKE. [What?] [Are what?]

KEVIN. [I can't put] [it into…]

BLAKE. [Fucking what!]

KEVIN. I don't know if I can stay with you if you have it.

(Pause. Then quickly trying to recover…)

And I think that's awful, but I don't know how that would work and I don't know what not knowing means, and I think that means something, do [you understand…?]

BLAKE. *(raising his hand to stop* **KEVIN***, wounded, stunned…)* [Palomino.]

(pause)

KEVIN. Blake, I know how it sounds, but it's [something to…]

BLAKE. [Please stop.]

KEVIN. I'm [only…]

BLAKE. [Jesus, just] stop talking!

(pause)

I'm not gonna' be "sick." And even if I…fuck, ugh, that doesn't mean whatever it, what it used to mean. I'm not gonna' need, look, don't fucking lecture me on not knowing anything and then act like you don't know anything because it's easier, because you're too scared to take some responsibility [for any of…]

KEVIN. [Responsibility?]

BLAKE. Kevin, the whole night, the whole thing was your, no. No. Look, I did what I did and I own it, okay? But when you sat there with your mouth shut and watched him fuck me right in front of you, just watched it happen, I feel stupid even trying to, why didn't you say something? Something besides "That's good!" How about "stop" or "hold on…?"

KEVIN. I didn't, it felt more real, watching, more right than trying to, like a, like in a video. It was really, I don't know, hot. And I guess I didn't say anything because I didn't…

*(***KEVIN*** *puts it together.)*

I didn't want it to stop.

(Pause. Something is broken.)

BLAKE. Is it still hot?

KEVIN. Baby, I'm trying to explain how it felt and [I know...]

(He is cut off by **BLAKE**'s *laughter.)*

BLAKE. [You sure] are good at explaining, you talk and talk. This isn't an explain moment. There's no undo now.

KEVIN. Blake, I know there's something I can say, something to help, make it better or, I [don't know.]

BLAKE. [Ya' know,] it's the strangest thing, listening to you, just sitting here, somewhere inside me right now there is a, something's screaming, I can hear it like it's far away, but I can't make it happen. I can't connect all of that inside me to this. It's so close, right here, but I can't seem to get at it. And I think, look at you, Jesus, look at you, if I could go back to that moment, that flash of time in the dark when I was getting fucked by two guys that you picked out while you were cowering a few feet away, if I could see your face at that moment, I wonder if it would look like it does right now?

KEVIN. I'm sorry.

BLAKE. Ugh, I think maybe it would.

KEVIN. I'm sorry.

BLAKE. Fuck you!

(pause)

I know you think you're sorry. You think a lot. I love you, Kevin, but right now I wish I could not; I wish I could make it stop.

KEVIN. Blake, I am sorry.

BLAKE. If you're sorry, and I don't know that you know what that really feels like, but if you're "sorry" then say it doesn't matter because it doesn't matter, that's the thing you're looking for, the thing you can say, right, because it's not the end of [the world.]

KEVIN. [And it's not] that fucking simple to just [turn everything...]

BLAKE. [You don't] even have to say it out loud, just whisper it in my ear. Just say it, I don't even know if you have to mean it, you can just say it.

(*Pause.* **KEVIN** *starts to cross to* **BLAKE**, *but he stops.*)

It's…almost like I should feel bad for you. For you. It's almost like that.

KEVIN. (*Shaking off the moment, he changes gears completely, something crazed slips into him.*) None of, none of this ocean stuff means anything, I mean it, it's bullshit. It's not, it's all, I think you're gonna' be fine.

BLAKE. You already said that.

KEVIN. You don't have it. You know, let's go, yes, let's go find Max, and he'll tell us where Andy is and we'll talk to them and you'll see it's all just a big, [stupid…]

BLAKE. [They] should tell you what kind of sea monster. It must be awful.

KEVIN. Are you coming?

BLAKE. Do you think Andy was scared?

KEVIN. Come with me.

BLAKE. No.

KEVIN. Fuck. Fuck, then I'll go find them and I'll, I'll drag them back here to you. And you'll see this is some kind of, I don't know.

BLAKE. Say you're sorry again.

KEVIN. I'm sorry.

BLAKE. For what?

KEVIN. I'm sorry that…

(*Pause.* **BLAKE** *smiles, but it's not a good thing.*)

BLAKE. You don't know, not even a little bit.

KEVIN. You're wrong. I'll be back soon, you'll see.

(*He exits.* **BLAKE** *picks the mashed up telegram up off the floor and smoothes it out. He looks at the door…*)

End Scene

7

(*Waves of blue lights again illuminate the apartment. Lights up on a small pool of water.* **MAX** *is sitting in it, knees pulled to his chest. He clutches a yellow telegram.*)

(**KEVIN** *enters in a rush.*)

KEVIN. Max? The door was open and, what in, what happened in here?

MAX. Nothing.

KEVIN. It's not [nothing.]

MAX. [It's nothing.]

KEVIN. Are you okay?

MAX. I told you we're having, I'm having trouble with the pipes.

KEVIN. This is, this is a [disaster.]

MAX. [Just get] the fuck out!

KEVIN. We got the, we got another telegram. Telegrams. About Andy. And Blake is getting all these ideas in his head, not just ideas something else, and I wanted to find you and Andy [to get...]

MAX. *(laughing)* [You want] you want [you want...]

KEVIN. [Will you,] will you just tell me where Andy is, where he really is?

MAX. Gone and gone and gone and I bet you never thought, flirting with us in a bar, bet you never thought anything like this. Because we were, we were so...something. We were something. I wish you could have seen how we were before all of this...

(*He waves the telegram.*)

KEVIN. It's not real.

MAX. It's not real? How can I...? My apartment, my apartment is under water, Kevin. My boyfriend went to the bottom of the ocean and was, he was killed by a sea monster. A fucking sea monster. Don't talk to me about what's real right now, because I have no sense of, I mean how do I [know?]

KEVIN. [Max,] it [can't be...]

MAX. [It's real.] It's fucking real. I don't know how, but it's real. And Andy is, he's...ya' know that guy, that "delivery boy" just handed this to me. He just handed it to me with a smile on his face. He smiled at me while he handed me this. And then he was gone. A shit-eating smile on his face. No, not even that, no cruelty, no sympathy, no underlying anything, like plastic.

KEVIN. What does it say?

MAX. I can't read it.

KEVIN. Do you want me to read it?

MAX. No, you fucking, I could read it. I just can't anymore. I don't know, it's all smudged now. I did read it, and then I dropped it in the water. And it got all...but I did read it. I just can't remember what it said. It was from Andy, but I can't remember what it said.

KEVIN. Can I see it?

MAX. The telegram?

KEVIN. Yes.

MAX. No. No, where's Blake?

KEVIN. At home.

MAX. Alone?

KEVIN. Yes.

MAX. You left him alone?

KEVIN. Why?

MAX. Is he okay?

KEVIN. He's fine.

MAX. No, is he, does he have it?

KEVIN. Does he, we, don't know anything yet; it takes time for anything [to show...]

MAX. [It's been] months.

KEVIN. It's, it's only been a little over a week since you [told me.]

MAX. [What are] you talking about?

KEVIN. Okay, I'm sure it's not good for you to be sitting in the water [like that.]

MAX. [Do you] have it?

KEVIN. No.

MAX. You know for sure?

KEVIN. Yes, I'm sure.

MAX. *(with a spark of recognition, a little laugh…)* Ah…I guess it's always safer when you only watch.

KEVIN. I didn't just watch. But then I got, all of the sudden, afraid. Just afraid.

MAX. Not just afraid though, right? Something else too.

KEVIN. I don't know what [you're…]

MAX. [Yes you] do. Yes. Something else held you there, kept your eyes open. Watching us. Sex is fascinating, isn't it? I'm sitting here mourning the loss of the closest thing I've ever had to true love, probably will ever have even remotely resembling true love, and I think I would feel so much better if someone just threw me against a wall, rough, and fucked me until I couldn't feel anything anymore. Fucked me until I was blinded by that base, sweet kind of anguish and I wouldn't be able to think of Andy not being here now. And I wouldn't be able to think of anything. And I would be empty and used and completely erased. Fucking erased. And I would let someone do that to me. I would and…that's fascinating.

(MAX looks him up and down like a predatory animal.)

You're not the one for that job though, are you? You'd want to fuck me and then you'd be afraid all of the sudden.

KEVIN. Look, look I'm sorry. I'm sorry if you're mad at me, or depressed or just going crazy, or whatever the fuck this is, but I really need to find [out…]

MAX. [I'm not] mad! I'm just an asshole, but that night, you on the edge scared to jump in, I think Blake was more afraid, in the middle of it, in the act of it, but then…he's a different kind of person, isn't he?

KEVIN. Than who?

MAX. Than us, than me and probably you. When Andy told me, I should have said that it didn't matter. Even though I don't really think that, even though it does. No, fuck, no it doesn't. I should have said it didn't matter; I should have felt that too.

KEVIN. You can't help it.

MAX. But I think sometimes, Kevin, look at me right now, sometimes when people say that, they really can help it. They just don't want to try.

KEVIN. I don't…Is there anything I can do [for you?]

MAX. [Can you] give me Andy back?

KEVIN. No, I [don't…]

MAX. [Can you] give me the last eight years back?

KEVIN. Max, you [shouldn't…]

MAX. [Can you] fucking stop all this water from coming back?! I keep trying to clean it up, and it keeps coming back. I can't make it stop. And it's not coming from anywhere in particular; it's just coming and coming and coming. It's not enough to drown in, but, to be completely fair, I haven't really tried that hard yet. We're all grown up now, we know all these things, and we should really learn how to finish what we start. You think?

KEVIN. You should come with me.

MAX. I'm not going anywhere.

KEVIN. I don't think you should be alone right now.

MAX. That's exactly what I should be. It's nothing; you should go.

(*The ROAR happens in the distance.* **MAX** *jerks his head up, springing into a crouch in the water.*)

Did you hear it?

KEVIN. Yes.

(**MAX** *slowly whistles the same tune that the* **TELEGRAM DELIVERY BOY** *whistled in his earlier appearances.* **KEVIN** *backs away.*)

MAX. You've got your own problems to deal with. Don't worry about me.

KEVIN. Max, I'm serious, [you need to…]

MAX. [It's nothing!]

(pause)

I'm nothing. Fix that. Nobody can fix that. I can't sink because there's nothing inside me. I'm like a rubber ducky; all I can do is quack and splash around. And feel sad. And not have Andy. And not…where's Blake?

KEVIN. I told you, he's at home.

MAX. Are you sure?

KEVIN. Yes.

MAX. I wouldn't be so sure. Don't worry though; it's nothing.

(MAX *begins slowly whistling the tune again.)*

KEVIN. Max?

(MAX *ignores him, splashing the water a bit.* **KEVIN** *exits quickly.)*

End Scene

8

(Waves of blue lights again illuminate the apartment. The main lights do not rise to illuminate the apartment. A small trickle of water seeps in through the open door, down the stairs and into the sunken area. A pool has formed in the living room.)

*(***KEVIN** *enters, rushing through the open door and down the stairs into calf-deep water. He stops and takes in the scene.)*

KEVIN. No. No.

(He rushes across the room towards the kitchen.)

Blake? Blake, are you here? I saw Max and I think I know…

(He moves into the kitchen. His voice comes from off stage…)

Blake!

(He enters the main room again in a rush and stops. The **TELEGRAM DELIVERY BOY** *appears at the door. It is open, so he knocks on the frame with a chipper smile, soaking wet from head to toe. A light filters in from behind him, illuminating the space, as water continues to seep in down the stairs.)*

TELEGRAM DELIVERY BOY. Good afternoon sir.

KEVIN. What the fuck is going on?

TELEGRAM DELIVERY BOY. I have a telegram for Mr. Kevin Richards.

KEVIN. Who's it from?

TELEGRAM DELIVERY BOY. Oh gosh, I'm sorry sir. Policy is we can't read the telegrams. Privacy and all? You'll have to read it yourself.

KEVIN. No, I, I don't want it.

TELEGRAM DELIVERY BOY. I'm sorry, sir, but you have to take it.

(He crosses down the stairs into the water without

hesitation or acknowledgment holding out the telegram.)

KEVIN. Where is he?

TELEGRAM DELIVERY BOY. Where is who?

KEVIN. I know you know what I'm talking about, where's Blake, where is he?

TELEGRAM DELIVERY BOY. Sir, I'm sorry, [but…]

KEVIN. [Where is] he?

TELEGRAM DELIVERY BOY. Why do you care?

(pause)

KEVIN. What?

TELEGRAM DELIVERY BOY. I'm sure if you'll just take this and read it, you'll understand.

KEVIN. Is it from him?

TELEGRAM DELIVERY BOY. Sir, I [don't…]

KEVIN. [Is it] from [Blake?]

TELEGRAM DELIVERY BOY. [I think] maybe you know who it's from?

KEVIN. I won't take it.

TELEGRAM DELIVERY BOY. Sir, we pride ourselves on customer service, but I'm afraid I have to insist that you take the…

*(*KEVIN *knocks the telegram out of his hand. It falls into the water.)*

I wonder sir, wonder with me for a minute, will you? I wonder if you can imagine what it's like to catch death as a small, tenacious little thing and hold it tight?

KEVIN. What [does this…?]

TELEGRAM DELIVERY BOY. [Hold it tight] because you can't let go of it, even if you want to, even when it gets larger and larger, becoming something that no one should ever have to see, you can't let it go. And then it looks at you. And you see what?

KEVIN. I just want to [know where…]

TELEGRAM DELIVERY BOY. [Come on,] what do you think you see when you're about to die?

KEVIN. I don't, a white light, why does [that even…?]

TELEGRAM DELIVERY BOY. *(laughing)* [A white light?]

KEVIN. Well what the fuck do [you see?]

TELEGRAM DELIVERY BOY. [You see] nothing. And then you die.

KEVIN. What is wrong with you?

TELEGRAM DELIVERY BOY. Not a thing in this big, blue world.

KEVIN. He might not even be sick!

TELEGRAM DELIVERY BOY. He might not even be sick?

KEVIN. You don't know for sure, he doesn't even know.

TELEGRAM DELIVERY BOY. *(astonished)* He might not even [be sick.]

KEVIN. [He might] be fine.

TELEGRAM DELIVERY BOY. You don't know.

KEVIN. That's right!

TELEGRAM DELIVERY BOY. Well gosh, sir, it doesn't matter.

(His eyes widen, something comes undone, his plastic persona vanishing like someone taking off a mask. His demeanor, posture, everything comes loose...)

It doesn't matter!!!

KEVIN. Because you don't think I want him [anymore.]

TELEGRAM DELIVERY BOY. [He doesn't] think you want [him anymore.]

KEVIN. [You think] I'll just read your stupid telegram and, you think I don't miss him, won't [miss him?]

TELEGRAM DELIVERY BOY. [Doesn't matter] what [I think.]

KEVIN. [I'll miss the] way he wakes up from an hour-long nap and looks like he was asleep for a thousand years, all groggy and his hair always sticking up. And how he changes cereals every week even though that is just the most infuriating thing. Or how he holds my hand under the table when we have dinner with my parents and my Dad makes that face he used to make when I didn't do well in soccer games. I'll miss how he knows within two notes everything that was ever recorded by any Icelandic pop band even though it all sounds like the same crushing depressive hum to me. I'll even miss the way he won't let me get a puppy, even though I beg and annoy him about it. Because, no matter what I promise, he knows I won't do a good job taking care of it. And he's right. I won't and he'll end up feeding it half the time, more than half the time, walking it. He knows I'm no good at, at taking...

TELEGRAM DELIVERY BOY. Ah, that's it, come on now, that's it right there. Almost got it, your irrational little hang up. Put it together. If you can't, even, take care, of a puppy, then how are you [going to...]

KEVIN. [Shut the] fuck [up!]

TELEGRAM DELIVERY BOY. [Ha! Which] is ridiculous, the idea that he would need you to "take care" of him, need you with some preposterous, fear-driven idea [you've concocted...]

KEVIN. [Oh my God, this] is, is, you're some kind of, of fucking nightmare.

(The ROAR sounds in the distance, closer than before but still far off. The **TELEGRAM DELIVERY BOY** *slams the door, shutting out the noise and the light. He takes out another telegram.)*

TELEGRAM DELIVERY BOY. No, that? That is a nightmare. That is what happens when people stop paying attention. I wish you could see it, look right at it. You know, it's mind boggling to me, can I just say? It defies belief that there can be this monstrosity thrashing around and making such a cacophonous racket, I mean it's nearly deafening, and somehow it's not there. Just step outside your door and listen, but no, no, people, people just...

(He makes a popping noise with his mouth.)

...wander around willfully ignorant of that. It's a gigantic monster and somehow it's always a surprise. Amazing! So no, that's what happens when people stop paying attention. I am what happens when people don't care. People like you. Now look, this is just a job. I don't have time to deal with your petty wallowing in, well, it seems like this is mostly your fault so I'm sure there are any number of things you can wallow in, but once you read this you'll feel better, or nothing, but that's better, now take it.

KEVIN. No.

TELEGRAM DELIVERY BOY. Take the telegram.

(KEVIN grabs it from his hand and immediately tears it up.)

KEVIN. For some reason, you're just not getting this: I'm not. Taking. Your message.

TELEGRAM DELIVERY BOY. Ugh. All right, let's try this:

(He shifts back into "plastic mode.")

Here's a simple question for you sir, in the wake of the heart-breaking puppy speech: do you love him?

KEVIN. What?

TELEGRAM DELIVERY BOY. Do you love [him?]

KEVIN. [Of course] I love him. I love him more than I've ever loved anyone.

TELEGRAM DELIVERY BOY. Great!

(He drops the "plastic mode.")

Too bad that's not enough. Love. Too bad it isn't just magic and that makes everything better. "I love you" and…

(He makes a popping noise with his mouth.)

…everything is spick and span.

KEVIN. You're wrong.

TELEGRAM DELIVERY BOY. And you're going to read one of these.

(He produces another telegram. KEVIN immediately crumples it up.)

KEVIN. Just give him back!

(The **TELEGRAM DELIVERY BOY** *takes off his hat and throws it on the chair. A warm blue glow begins to throb on the walls...)*

TELEGRAM DELIVERY BOY. You think I can do that? Just [like that?]

KEVIN. [You took] him, just give him back.

TELEGRAM DELIVERY BOY. No.

KEVIN. You can't just take people away [from the ones...]

TELEGRAM DELIVERY BOY. [I don't] take anybody. I'm just the guy that delivers the telegrams, I'm an infinitesimally small piece of something you couldn't begin to wrap your head around. The people that go, the ones like Blake, they choose to go, because they get thrown away.

KEVIN. That's not what happened.

TELEGRAM DELIVERY BOY. Oh really?

KEVIN. No.

TELEGRAM DELIVERY BOY. You are just unbelievable. Okay. Hold on; let me find it here, just the highlights, the pages stick together sometimes when they get wet...

(producing a notebook from his pocket, flipping through the pages)

Here we go, here's a priceless moment, you said:

(He reads quickly, without emotion, like minutes at a meeting.)

"I don't know if I can stay with you if you have it. And I think that's awful, but I don't know how that would work and I don't know what not knowing means, and I think that means something." Sound familiar?

KEVIN. How, how did [you...?]

TELEGRAM DELIVERY BOY. [Ugh, that's] confusing just to read out loud. And it's certainly not what I would call "reassuring," I would hardly call it a concrete [decision to...]

KEVIN. [You're totally] taking that, that out of context,

I mean, you have to be practical about things when they're uncertain, or, no, that sounds, you have to look at the big picture, things go through your [mind and...]

TELEGRAM DELIVERY BOY. [No, you, you're the] one that has to be "practical," look at the big picture. Blake has a very small picture right now; his picture is smaller by the minute and he gets to be afraid alone because the one person who should be afraid for him is afraid of him. And how about this little gem:

(*He flips a page and closes in on* **KEVIN**...)

"I didn't want it to stop." You looked right at him and said: "I didn't want it to stop." At that moment you could have said anything and you said: "I didn't want it to stop." That's just the worst [kind of...]

KEVIN. [Who the] fuck, no, who are you to, to cast judgment on, ya' know, you and that thing out there, it's all so easy isn't it? No, it's not just [black and white.]

TELEGRAM DELIVERY BOY. [You think] this is easy! Do you have any idea of the intensity, of the white-hot rage that burns through every tiny part of me when I have to hand someone one of these telegrams? When I have to fight with people, people like you, people that have fucked up and can't figure it out, can't see past this.

(*He motions to his uniform.*)

Pay attention. This is for you, all of this: the quaint uniform, the polite demeanor, the nostalgia of a telegram. Please, people don't even send telegrams anymore. It's all for you.

KEVIN. Why?

TELEGRAM DELIVERY BOY. Because you don't get a happy ending. There's no happy ending now. You get some small comfort and that's it. That's it.

KEVIN. Fuck that, because you say so?

TELEGRAM DELIVERY BOY. No, fucking listen, because it's already done.

(*He produces another telegram.*)

Now you take this and you read it.

KEVIN. Give him back you son of a bitch!

(*KEVIN rushes the* **TELEGRAM DELIVERY BOY**, *tackling him. A low rumble begins as the two men wrestle in the shallow water.*)

TELEGRAM DELIVERY BOY. None of this makes a difference. What's done is [done.]

KEVIN. [I won't] let him go!

TELEGRAM DELIVERY BOY. And what are you going to do if you get him back? You'll just get scared and leave him [again.]

KEVIN. [Fuck] you!

TELEGRAM DELIVERY BOY. It's who you are, it's written all over you, in everything you do. If you really wanted him here, I wouldn't be here!

(*The* **TELEGRAM DELIVERY BOY** *throws* **KEVIN** *across the room, sending him splashing down. The rumble continues to grow.* **KEVIN** *is on his back, he props himself up on his elbows, breathing heavy.*)

KEVIN. I love him!

TELEGRAM DELIVERY BOY. Just keep saying it. Ya' know, those are the easiest words to say, there's no trick to it, they're just words. People act like it's this huge thing, but they're just sounds that roll right off your lips. And it's always such a shock. You know what? He could hear you right now if he tried, if he wanted to hear you. He could be here right now, really, right this minute, bam just appear, if he believed you at all. If he believed you enough to really listen through the waves and the water and the quiet. But those words, they don't mean anything coming from you, and he knows it and that's why I'm still here and Blake's not.

(*He looms over* **KEVIN**. *Pulling his head back by the hair…*)

KEVIN. [Ugh.]

TELEGRAM DELIVERY BOY. [Now] just. Give. Up.

KEVIN. Do you, do you hear that?

(quiet and fast, growing into revelation...)

I have to keep, keep it, I can't stop, like someone pulling out my insides through a tiny hole in my chest, everything spilling out, he's getting out, I have to stop it, he has to know. I can see his face, I, I can see him looking at me, even now, right now, I can feel how he fits with me, against me, and nothing can [change that.]

TELEGRAM DELIVERY BOY. [Doesn't make] [a difference.]

KEVIN. [Doesn't] make a difference that I love him? Fuck you. Not like fucking movies and stories, not like poetry, what I feel is more than all that, it hurts, it's like my ribs imploding, breaking and crushing me, cutting up everything, it's wet and dirty, it's all over me, it's insane, it's fucking insane, I feel like I'm losing my mind, no, he needs me, he doesn't need to be alone, he needs to be here, where he [belongs and...]

TELEGRAM DELIVERY BOY. [I said] [Give up!]

KEVIN. [Where he belongs!] With me, and he knows it. You know it, Blake, can you hear me? You were right, I'm sorry, okay? And I won't let [you go.]

TELEGRAM DELIVERY BOY. [Just take] the telegram, [take it.]

KEVIN. *(Knocking the* **TELEGRAM DELIVERY BOY***'s hand away.)* [I won't!] It's my fault he's gone now, I get it; I know it. I'm sorry, Blake, sorry I didn't know, wanted more, that I was scared and weak and reckless with what we had, have, what we still have. No, so no matter what you do, I won't take that telegram. He needs to know that. Whatever happens, you, all of this, it doesn't matter, none of it, and I love him and those aren't just words and he's the reason that they're not just words so you can go deliver that message straight to the bottom of the god damned ocean and give him back!

(To the sky, to the sounds around him...)

Do you hear me! I will not let you go!

(The rumble grows loud enough to shake the stage, mixing with waves crashing.)

(The front door bursts open and a rush of water washes **BLAKE** *on, leaving him face down at the base of the stairs.* **KEVIN** *rushes to him and turns him over, pulling him up onto the stairs a bit, as the sounds subside. The natural lighting of the living room finally returns as the blue light fades.* **KEVIN** *taps* **BLAKE**'s *face trying to rouse him; he listens to his chest and then checks his airway. He lifts* **BLAKE** *up a bit. Suddenly* **BLAKE** *convulses, coughing, spitting up water, head tilted back, struggling for air.* **KEVIN** *holds him. The* **TELEGRAM DELIVERY BOY** *takes in the scene.)*

TELEGRAM DELIVERY BOY. Doesn't happen very often.

BLAKE. *(Still recovering, choking on the words, on the water…)*I heard you and…you better…you better mean all of…

KEVIN. I know,Bbaby, I did, I do.

(The **TELEGRAM DELIVERY BOY** *places the telegram back inside his shirt pocket, picks up his hat, moves to the door, but stops.)*

TELEGRAM DELIVERY BOY. You know…this doesn't mean he won't be sick.

KEVIN. But he's not alone.

(The **TELEGRAM DELIVERY BOY** *tips his hat with a smirk.)*

TELEGRAM DELIVERY BOY. We'll see.

(He snaps back into plastic mode.)

Have a nice day sir.

(He exits, whistling a little tune. The door is left open to the world.)

*(***KEVIN** *and* **BLAKE** *look at each other and kiss. The* ROAR *sounds in the distance.* **BLAKE** *jerks, looking toward the sound, afraid, but* **KEVIN** *gently pulls him back into the embrace.)*

End Play

Also by
Steve Yockey...

Bright. Apple. Crush.

Cartoon

Please visit our website **samuelfrench.com** for complete
descriptions and licensing information

From the Reviews of
OCTOPUS...

"A fiercely imaginative and finely tuned new voice...Smartly observed and blissfully performed...[*Octopus*'] tentacles tickle the funny bone, awake the mind and tug on the heart."
- San Francisco Chronicle

"An evening full of arresting images...classic tragedy seen through a very contemporary ironic lens"
- Marin Independent Journal

"This tale of two gay couples' group sex fling and its serious consequences arrives at a powerful statement about illness and love."
-Variety

"*Octopus* moves from naturalism to something strange and surreal, taking a high-risk gamble with audience acceptance that pays off at nearly the last possible minute...*Octopus* affirms Yockey's boldness in venturing into uncharted theatrical waters."
- Creative Loafing Atlanta